The Stain in the Stairwell

Published by A.P. Sessler
© 2017 by A.P. Sessler

Front Cover Art: Marcus Marritt www.marcusmarritt.com

eBook License Notes

The right of A.P. Sessler to be identified as the author of this work has been asserted by him in accordance with the Copyright, Designs and Patents Act 1988.

All Rights Reserved Worldwide. No part of this eBook may be reproduced or transmitted in any form without written consent from the publisher.

The characters and story in this eBook are purely fictitious. Any likeness to any person, living or dead, is purely coincidental. Except the Stain--that thing is real and will totally eat your face, dude.

THANKS

To editor Scarlett R. Algee, against whose better and more sensitive judgment I've decided to keep Cindy and Braden's affectation.

To the guys who answered lots of annoying questions how to jump into this whole publishing thing: Mark Parker, Mark Lumby and Jud Ghilotti.

To all those who know what it's like living on half a broken shoestring. It's not easy needing green.

eBOOKS BY A.P. SESSLER

The Stain in the Stairwell
The First Suitor
Brain Attack

AND ON PAPERBACK
House of the Goat

THE STAIN IN THE STAIRWELL

Emma submerged a jam-smeared plate beneath the soapy froth of the filling sink. She reached through the foamy surface to retrieve the dishrag and ran it in clockwise circles over the plate until the red raspberry stain disappeared.

The wail of a siren drew her attention to the window just above the sink, where outside and eight stories below an ambulance drove down the busy street behind the rundown apartment building, all in miniature like a living diorama. Her gaze ran up the sidewalk to the back entrance, where they stumbled upon a memory that made her shudder.

"Nattie?" she called as she rinsed the dish off.

The nine-year-old pushed her lavender-sleeved arms through the straps of her zebra-striped backpack. "What, Mom?"

Emma turned the faucet off and placed the plate in the dish drain. "I want you to use the railing on your way down the stairs from now on."

"I'm not a little girl, Mom."

"Yes, dear, you are. You're not a baby, but you're still a little girl. But that's beside the point. Hold on to the railing so you won't fall."

"I've never fallen before."

"*Fallen*. And that's beside the point, too. I don't want you winding up in the hospital because you didn't listen to Mommy."

"Are you afraid I'll breaked my neck like Missus Echo?"

Emma gasped, then swept her display of fear beneath a thin smile. "How did you hear about that?"

"The kids at the bus stop."

Emma had hoped Natalie hadn't heard the story at all, let alone from other children. "Yes, I am afraid. So can you make Mommy feel better by doing what she asks?"

Natalie sighed. "Okay."

"Thank you, sweetie."

Natalie shuffled across the small kitchen, the cuffs of her mauve corduroys brushing the linoleum tile. She opened the pantry door. A box of individually packaged puddings of varying flavors stood out on the middle shelf.

She swung the door back and forth. "Since I'm gonna hold on to the rail from now on, can I trade my apple for a extra pudding at snack time?"

"Nice try, Nattie. No."

Natalie's shoulders dropped with all the disappointment a child could display. "Aww."

Emma kept her amusement to herself. She dried her hands on a towel and knelt to one knee with open arms. "Come give me a kiss before you leave for school."

Natalie ran into the hug and exchanged freckled cheek kisses with her. Mother and daughter shared auburn hair—Emma, thick, shoulder-length; Natalie, a fine, girlish bob.

Emma smiled, brushing a silken lock of hair out of Natalie's brown eyes. "Good girl. See you later."

"'Kay."

When Natalie turned to walk away, Emma patted her backpack to ensure it was zipped shut. Emma followed her to the door and watched her walk down the long hall, past the broken-down elevator with the OUT OF SERVICE sign taped to it, to the door leading to the fire escape stairs.

The door slowly swung shut behind Natalie. The stairwell, as far as she could see down, was a wall of white, sterile, cold concrete. A fat snake of pipe clung to the walls, joined by a brood of smaller snakes, all concealed in chameleon skin cloaked white, their forms segmented by the occasional gauge or valve.

The big one gurgled some undigested meal--Natalie couldn't tell if it was coming up or going down. Elsewhere along the walls stood a meter or box or panel, also camouflaged in white.

She had made it from the landing and down the first section of metal stair when she remembered her mother's words. When she placed her hand on the cold railing, reflex drew it back. She pulled her long shirt sleeve over a cupped hand and made a second attempt to obey her mother.

Turn by turn she descended the flight of stairs till she reached the first floor. When her sleeve snagged on a patch of rusted rail, she pulled her hand back once more and descended the remainder of the steps, disregarding her mother's orders.

It was quiet save for the hum of the cooler in the drink machine by the door, that and a curious *drip-drip* echo coming from somewhere. She glanced beneath the drink machine, expecting to find a pooling puddle, but instead found a plastic glue trap featuring an assortment of many-legged dead things: a silverfish, a wolf spider and its scattered, trapped young, and two cockroaches—one of them still squirming to escape from its sticky situation. Natalie's stomach squirmed right along with the grotesque insect.

Her attention was diverted to a row of M&Ms behind the glass of the other vending machine. How many dollars' worth of change she and the kids had put into that thing: nabs, peanuts, potato chips, candy bars. Surely Mr. Ferelli had to be rich by now.

She heard the drip-drip again but chose to ignore it. She approached the metal-framed glass door just past the vending machines and placed a hand on the glass. Outside she observed the lone sidewalk, where an ugly-green metal bench and small octagonal sign stood signifying the bus stop. The four schoolmates who usually accompanied her were strangely absent.

She looked as far along the sidewalk as her angle permitted. The small flight of concrete stairs leading to the front entrance was occupied, but not by classmates. Two men with sagging pants puffed on cigarettes and blew smoke in the air, engaged in a conversation she couldn't hear.

She turned and looked up the stairs, straining to hear what she thought might be approaching footsteps, but it was only the drip-drip she had noticed earlier. Turning back, she saw the fat metal snake she walked alongside every morning and afternoon had apparently been swimming, as the bottom of its tail seemed to be the source of the constant dripping.

The ground-floor wall behind the metal structures was covered in an ugly red-brown shape. Natalie went up the first few steps of the metal stair to the landing feeding to the next succession of stairs. She looked at the ugly stain, how it had so quickly turned the bleach-white wall she knew into a colorful curiosity.

She reached out to touch it.

Honk!

She spun around. Outside, the rumbling school bus idled. She hurried down the stairs, out of the apartment and up onto the bus. The driver closed the doors behind her, and after a grind of gears the bus disappeared.

In the quiet stairwell, the drip-drip became a trickle, then another, then another, and soon it sounded like a running faucet. Water slowly pooled upon the landing beneath the stairs.

Natalie exited the bus alone and entered the stairwell lobby. The mysterious leak had resumed its calm drip-drip. A yellow plastic folding sign placed on the landing read WET FLOOR, and displayed a cartoon of a stick man slipping on the floor, off his feet, into the air like it had been covered with a careless clown's discarded banana peel. Oddly enough, everywhere she looked, the floor seemed bone-dry.

When she remembered her mother's words about falling, she took hold of the rusted railing, forgetting how cold the metal was. She folded her sleeve around her hand and made her way up to the first landing.

There was the stain again. She approached the wall. The stain had grown wider since that morning, but not up. Looking straight down between the wall and stair, she could see it had spread onto the floor beneath the landing.

What was that ugly stuff? Poop? Blood? What else could it be, that ugly red-brown? She reached out and with a single finger, wiped the wall, expecting a white smudge to appear. The only thing that changed color was her finger; it was now the same ugly red-brown as the wall.

"Yuck," she said with a scowl and wiped it on her shirt.

The drip-drip turned into a trickle. She returned to the railing and, obeying her mother, kept her covered hand on it until she exited the stairwell to her floor.

She made her way to her apartment door, where she entered her passcode on the keyless entry system. A tiny light turned green and the door unlocked. When she pulled the door shut behind her, the deadbolt engaged and the little light turned red.

"Hi, honey," Emma's voice greeted her.

"Hi," Natalie said, pulling her arms free from her backpack to place it on the wingback chair in the living room.

A continual knock-knock came from the kitchen. Natalie imagined a little man inside the pantry door begging to come out.

Emma's head popped from behind the kitchen corner. "How was school?"

"Okay," said Natalie, stepping into the kitchen.

Emma was busy chopping a yellow bell pepper with a large butcher knife atop a cutting board. "Did you hold on to the railing up and down the stairs like Mommy told you?"

"Yes, ma'am," she answered, and wondered if it was a lie that she hadn't held it where it was rusty and jagged.

"Were all the children okay being at the bus stop? With Mrs. Eckhart's accident and all, I mean."

"Nobody came today."

The chopping stopped. "Nobody what?"

"I was the only one there."

"You were the only one at the bus stop?"

Natalie nodded.

Emma laid the knife flat on the counter. "You were there by yourself?"

"Mmm-hmm." Natalie nodded again.

"No one else showed up? You were all alone?"

Natalie ignored the third attempt at clarification, choosing instead to answer the nagging hunger in her stomach by going to the pantry in search of an acceptable snack. She opened the pantry door. No little man anywhere in sight. That made it much easier to find the peanut butter and bread.

"Can I have a sandmich before dinner?" she asked.

Emma stood with one hand on her hip, her shoulders hunched and mouth and eyes half-open. "Nuh-uh, I don't think so."

"Please?"

"We've been here for three months. They're not going to keep treating us like lepers," said Emma, poking a curled finger to accent her desired syllables.

She stood straight and reached for her cell phone.

"I'll only eat half," Natalie appealed.

She heard a tap-tap. It reminded her of the drip-drip. It was Emma's shoe on the kitchen tile. Natalie closed the pantry door and went to the living room couch. She took the TV remote from the coffee table and within a few clicks brought afternoon cartoons on-screen at near-full volume.

"Natalie!" Emma scolded her.

Natalie shrank into the couch and turned the volume too low to hear. She tried to read the character's lips, to no avail, but regardless she was mesmerized by the animated images. She watched the assortment of characters carry on, her mother's voice the only dialog.

"Hi, Gloria ... Emma ... Did you take Antwon and Cherise to school today? ... Okay, I just found Natalie was the only one at the bus stop ... She was? I didn't get a text, an email, nothing ... I don't blame you; I know you're busy with all their after-school activities ... Thanks for letting me know ... Have a good night. Bye."

A series of soft beeps.

"Monique? ... It's Emma. I just got off the phone with Gloria and found out you were supposed to tell me no one would be at the bus stop today ... Well, you can take that up with her, but at the moment that's beside the point ... Well, you should make time. Natalie sat there all by herself today ... No, *obviously* it's my problem ... Yeah? Maybe you need to check *yourself* 'cause this white girl can go from soccer mom to ghetto bitch in two seconds. You know what I'm saying? ... Yeah? ... And you, too!"

There was an angry sigh and several deep breaths, then another series of beeps. After listening to the recorded message, she left one herself.

"Hi Cindy, this is Emma. Sorry to miss you. I just found out Natalie was at the bus stop all by herself today. Apparently I didn't get the memo, so in the future can you please keep me in the loop so my daughter isn't a sitting duck to every pedophile and kidnapper? Thank you."

She hung up the phone with an exasperated sigh. "Busy talking to Monique, I'm sure."

Natalie's stare demanded her attention. When it was gained, Emma saw she wore a frown.

"What's wrong, baby?" Emma asked.

Natalie stood by the couch, shoulders drooping. "The kids are gonna be mad at me," she pouted.

"No they won't, baby. Their moms are going to be mad at me. And if any of them talk bad to you, you tell Mommy and I will personally kick their asses. 'Kay?"

Natalie snickered. "You're not 'sposed to swear, Mommy."

"I know, baby. I'm sorry. What they did was very wrong and it made Mommy very mad. I won't do it again, 'kay?"

"You promise?"

Emma laughed as her eyes teared. "No."

Natalie approached her with open arms. "I still love you."

Emma embraced her. "Still?"

"Mmm-hmm."

Emma squeezed her tight. "I never would have made you stay there by yourself had I known."

"It's okay. I'm not a baby."

"I know," Emma laughed and released her. "Now go wash up. Dinner's gonna be ready soon."

"No peanut butter sandmich?"

"You'll ruin your appetite."

"Okay," Natalie said and made her way to the living room and turned right down the hall.

She passed her bedroom on the left and took the bathroom door on the right. She pushed the light switch up. A sink-mirror combo sat left, the toilet to the right, and the shower against the far wall.

Drip-drip. She watched the droplets fall from the mirror steel faucet, then stood on her toes and peered into the endless black of the drain at the bottom of the white ceramic sink.

Emma sliced the carrot into increasingly smaller discs. *Chop-chop*. A whole tomato and broccoli crown sat beside a bowl of fresh, hand-torn romaine. *Chop-chop-chop--*

"Mom!" Natalie shouted.

Emma's stopped mid-chop, her heart in her throat. "Nattie? Are you okay?" she called.

It was silent. Emma dried her hands on a towel and stepped into the living room.

"Do you think Missus Echo will haunt the building?" Natalie hollered and poked her head out of the bathroom.

Emma stared hopelessly at the ceiling and sighed. "No, honey. Mrs. Eckhart isn't a ghost."

"Is she an angel?"

"I don't know, honey."

"The kids say she's a ghost," she said and disappeared into the bathroom.

Emma shook her head. "Damn brats."

Emma held on to the railing, with Natalie one or two steps behind in a yellow raincoat as they descended the stairs to the ground floor hand-in-hand. Voices chirped from far below, like a nest of baby birds awaiting morning worms, but rising above their chirp-chirp was the drip-drip.
    They hadn't reached the first floor when Natalie observed the red-brown stain had risen higher. She gazed up at the fat metal snake caught mid-slither across the rancid slick. Though it and its brood lay perfectly still, fastened to the wall like an entomologist's butterfly collection, they seemed to wind and coil with each corner.
    "Ow!" said Emma, pulling back her hand to find a sliced finger. "Stupid rail."
    Natalie had intended to warn her mother about the rusted rail, but was distracted by the metal snakes. "Sorry, Mom."
    "It wasn't your fault," Emma said, retrieving a band-aid from her purse.
    On the ground-floor landing they found Natalie's classmates. Their mothers stood just outside the door beneath the narrow green awning that kept them dry from the falling drizzle.
    Monique, slim and fit, was not unattractive. Face India ink-black with yarn dreads, two feet long, violet and black, woven among hair extensions of like length. A purple tubetop cupped her small bust, while tight black spandex pants revealed her more ample side.
    Cindy wore her blond hair in a pony tail. Her pitted egg-white face and spacious teeth confessed to substance abuse. Black tattooed names in various scripts marked her neck, wrist and back. A small paunch hung out of her short white tank-top just over the belt loops of her tight blue jeans.
    The two chatted and smoked cigarettes, while the plump Gloria stood a few feet away, hands crossed at the waist, her back and one foot against the wall. Even when she didn't smile, her cherubic face was friendly. She wore her hair short, straightened bangs long, black against brown skin.
    When Emma peeked through the door, Gloria waddled inside the lobby penguin-style to greet her. "Girl, you don't wanna hear what they been saying about you," she warned.
    Emma rolled her eyes. "I can only imagine."
    Gloria looked at Natalie, though she addressed Emma. "I'm so sorry no one told you yesterday."

"It's okay. I know you have my back."

"It's a shame about Mrs. Eckhart."

"Yes, it is."

"Antwon and Cherise are half-scared to be here. They keep going on about the ghost."

"I know. Natalie asked yesterday if Mrs. Eckhart was going to haunt the building."

"No, not Mrs. Eckhart," Gloria said, her voice changing to a whisper. "The ghost that killed her."

Emma's eyes widened. "Natalie, why don't you go stand with the children."

"'Kay, Mom. Love you," she said and walked off to join the children by the vending machines.

The portly Antwon and sister Cherise greeted her with smiles. Braden, Cindy's son, stood aloof. Kanisha, Monique's daughter, marched up to Natalie at once.

"My mama said your mama shouldn't live here," said Kanisha, her finger in Natalie's chest.

"Why?" asked Natalie.

"'Cause she rich."

"We're not rich."

"She got some fancy job."

"But we're not rich."

"Y'all think you're better than everyone."

"Quit it," said Cherise. "She ain't bothering no one."

Kanisha spun around. "Butt out. Ain't no one talking to you."

"Well, I'm talking to you. Leave her alone," said Cherise.

Kanisha pushed Cherise. "Make me."

Braden's jaw dropped.

Antwon stepped between his sister and Kanisha, his chest puffed out. "Push her again," he said, his soft voice deepening.

Braden stepped back and looked away. Kanisha bit her lip and crossed her arms. A moment later she stomped off. Braden followed a few steps behind, but her dirty look made him give pause.

"Siccing your big brother on me like a little chicken," she mumbled.

"Thanks, guys," said Natalie.

"Aw, she ain't nothing," said Antwon.

Kanisha walked up to the next landing, just as Emma walked past her to return upstairs. Emma offered a polite smile only to get a mock version, and turned back in return.

"Brat," said Emma.

Natalie watched their interaction from afar. She listened to her mother's footsteps, and as they grew softer, the drip-drip of the water grew louder in her tiny ears.

The two women stepped inside from the rain to meet Gloria, Monique patting her hair to remove any dampness.

"Why you talking to her?" Monique asked.

"The question should be, why *aren't* you?" said Gloria.

Monique huffed. "You getting awful friendly all the sudden."

"I'm feeling less prone by the moment," Gloria retorted.

"What's that mean?"

"It means what it means."

"Well, then."

"*Well, then* is right. Give the girl a break. Tired of y'alls' triflin'. Just because she got her act half-way together, y'all jealous."

Monique planted a hand on her hip. "Hmm."

Gloria crossed her arms and looked away. "Hmm."

Natalie couldn't stand eavesdropping any longer. She wandered toward the stairs, where the drip-drip grew louder still. She glanced up to find Kanisha looking down upon her. Natalie tried to force a friendly smile. With a huff, Kanisha looked away.

The drip-drip became a trickling sound. Natalie looked over her shoulder to see a tiny stream running down the wall. She gazed up at the stream to find its source, only to lose sight of it after a few floors.

She reached out to touch the narrow stream. The closer her fingers came, the stronger the trickle flowed, the wider it grew. A smile spread across her face when she thought of a purring cat.

Kanisha leaned against the railing, inches from the wall, unaware a branch of the red-brown stain had separated from the wall like loose wallpaper. She only noticed when it folded overhead like a big floppy leaf, just before it dropped onto her face. A sizzling sound drew Natalie's eyes upward once more.

Kanisha pulled at the fold of substance to remove it, but its burning grip made her let loose. "Mama!" she cried.

At her call Monique came stumbling in her heels, nearly twisting her ankle as she made her way up the stairs. "What is it, baby?"

"The stain," Kanisha cried with her face buried in her hands. "It got me."

Monique looked at the wall. The stain stood there, flat against the wall, motionless, as most stains do. "What you talking 'bout, baby?"

"It got me," Kanisha said, weeping.

Monique knelt to one knee and took her by the shoulders. "It's all right, baby. Ain't nothing got you but me. I'm here now."

"It *did* get me. Ask Natalie."

Monique glanced down at Natalie, who stood quietly, staring up, coldly detached from the moment. Natalie withdrew her hand from the wall.

Gloria and Cindy stood on the landing.

"She owright?" Cindy asked. "Is everything okay?" said Gloria.

Monique glanced over her shoulder. "She's fine," she said and pulled at Kanisha's hand. "Let me look at you."

"No!" Kanisha shouted and turned away.

"Come on, baby. Let Mama see."

Kanisha turned to her, her face still hidden in her hands. Monique ran her left hand across her back to comfort her.

"That's it," said Monique as she reached for Kanisha's hand.

Her eye was red from crying. Tears ran down her ebony cheek.

Monique held her hand. "See. You all right, baby. Now stop crying."

Kanisha lowered her other hand.

Monique gasped and let go of her. "Oh God. Oh Jesus. Oh Lord Jesus."

"What, Mama?" Kanisha asked.

Monique's half-open jaw trembled. Her hands shook, too afraid to touch her own child, even if to comfort her.

Gloria and Cindy ascended the first steps when they saw.

"Dear Lord," said Gloria and cupped her mouth with her hand.

"Oh sh--" Cindy stopped herself, taking the back of her hand to her lips.

Kanisha's color, from forehead to cheek, was gone. The pigment had been stripped, bleached from her skin. Only a raised, raw-red edge remained, separating albino white from ebony black.

"What is it, Mama?" she said, reaching for her mother.

Monique winced at her touch. Her mouth twisted into a speechless, sorrowful grimace. She wailed with each long breath, filling the entire stairwell, bottom to top, with her reverberating cries.

The children exited the bus and stood stock still on the sidewalk stop, their hesitant faces glaring back at them from the glass door between them and the haunted stairwell.

Somehow Antwon found himself volunteering to walk point, the rest falling behind to prod him forward. He glanced left. A moment later he glanced right. Their eyes followed every minute movement.

He glanced left again. Then right a second time. He calculated his options. With hopeful eyes, the tiny troop waited on his lead.

"I ain't going in there," he said, shaking his head.

"How we s'posed to get home?" asked Braden.

Antwon put his hands on his hips. "How you think? The front door."

"But the elevator doesn't work. 'Member?" said Natalie.

Antwon turned away in deep reflection.

"We can go tru da front doe den go to da side doe," Braden suggested.

"We still have to go up the stairs," said Cherise.

Braden's mouth dropped open in realization, then he gazed at his feet. "I forgot." His head shot up. "Den we gonna hafta run."

The portly siblings sighed, knowing they could easily break a sweat scaling the stairs at a moderate pace. Braden couldn't help but imagine the two providing the ghost a moment's amusement, offering him the perfect window of time to escape unscathed.

The door swung shut.

The three children stared at Natalie, just behind the glass.

"She crazy," said Braden.

With another sigh the siblings followed suit, until Braden was the only one standing outside. "All y'all crazy," he said, and joined them in the stairwell.

Natalie stood on the first floor landing. "Come on, y'all. It's safe. It won't hurt us, see?" She wore a confident smile, her arms outstretched.

The three children below faced one another, then Braden's gaze fell to his feet. "Maybe we should...hode hands...or sometin."

Antwon's lips puckered in consideration. "Okay," he said, extending a hand to either side.

Cherise took one, Braden the other.

Cherise held out her hand. "Natalie?"

Natalie was distracted by the deep, deep stain. "Huh?" she asked, facing her friend.

"Grab my hand. We gonna go up the stairs."

Natalie glanced back at the wall, then the hand. "I think I'm gonna stay a minute."

"What? You crazy!" said Braden.

"You sure?" said Cherise.

Natalie nodded. "I'll be okay."

Antwon's brow raised. "Okay. But you shout if you in trouble," he said, immediately praying beneath his breath. "Lord, please don't let her need help." Despite his single mother's excellent parenting skills, he sometimes hated his chivalrous ways.

Natalie watched the three climb up the stairs, growing ever smaller with each step. Unseen doors swung shut on creaking hinges. She glanced down the stairwell to ensure she was alone, and she was, just as she wished.

"Are you the ghost that killed Missus Echo?" she asked, facing the wall.

The brown stream bubbled and popped.

"Why did you kill her? Was she bad?"

The stream narrowed and ran quicker.

"That's okay. You don't have to say."

She walked up a few steps, admiring the sheer size of the massive stain.

"I saw what you did to Kanisha. I was right there," she said, her voice turning to a whisper. "She deserved it."

The stream widened again, and bubbled and popped. Natalie stretched a curious hand toward the moving water. To her awe, a soccer ball-sized portion of the stain peeled off the wall and flopped over.

"Do you want to shake my hand?" she asked, but it only bubbled.

She opened her palm to receive the fingerless "hand" when it shot for her raincoat.

She gasped in alarm. "Let go," she demanded, attempting to wrestle free.

It tugged at her but she tugged back. With her free hand she pulled the vinyl sleeve out of the stain's grip. The flat hand lashed out again, catching her sweater by the wrist.

Her eyes widened as the smoldering threads of her sleeve unwound, withering into smoke.

"Help!" she cried and jerked her arm free, the cuff of her sweater parting with her sleeve into the stain's dissolving acid grip.

She ran up the stairs, as far from the wall and the stain's reach as possible, pounding her knees and knuckles and fingers into the cold steel balusters all the way up. She shoved the fire escape door open and immediately shoved it shut from the other side.

With heaving breaths she dared to peek through the door's tiny window, an ecliptic glimpse into a caged nightmare. The stain inched up the wall, its gurgling, bubbling voice echoing through the stairwell. She pushed the door again to ensure it was shut and hurried to her apartment.

The door opened. Natalie turned back, holding the door. She looked down the hallway, expecting the monster to come bursting through the stairwell door and rushing toward her, but it didn't. Nothing happened; still, something told her she'd better shut the door, so she did.

Light from the computer monitor shone on Emma's face. In the screen, she saw Natalie's silhouette. She spun in her chair and saw the terrified look on her daughter's face. She leaped from the chair and ran to Natalie, kneeling before her to examine her.

"What happened?" Emma asked, holding Natalie's hands in her palms, the torn skin over her little knuckles all bloody.

"I ran into the rail on the stairs."

Emma noticed the torn sleeve. She tugged at it. "What happened to your sweater, Nattie?"

Natalie's lower lip trembled. "The monster got me."

Emma's chest swelled with an angry breath. "What monster? Did Mr. Ferelli touch you?"

Natalie's shoulders sunk. "No, Mama. The monster!"

"Honey, I don't know what you mean. Did one of the kids at school do this? Was it Braden?"

"It was the monster on the wall. The brown, yucky monster on the stairs."

Emma shook her head. "Show me."

Natalie looked aside. "I don't wanna."

"Nattie, you have to show me."

Natalie's tiny chest heaved with silent sobs. "But it'll get me."

"Nothing will get you with Mommy there."

Natalie looked aside again. "It got Kanisha when her mom was there."

Emma tried not to roll her eyes. "Just show me."

Natalie stood just inside the stairwell, her hand on the handle, ready to exit at any sign of danger.

"There." She pointed. "The brown monster."

Emma glanced back and forth before she realized. "The stain? You mean the stain on the wall?"

Natalie nodded and wrung her hands. "Please come back before it gets you, Mama."

Emma looked up in a hopeless, silent prayer. "It's just a stain, Nattie. See?" she said and poked the stain.

Natalie's heart froze as Emma's finger stroked the ferocious, sleeping beast.

"No!" Natalie screamed.

"Shh. Quiet, honey."

Stomping footsteps echoed in the stairwell from below.

"What the hell is going on up there?" a voice shouted.

Natalie and Emma peeked over the rail to see Mr. Ferelli peeking right back up from the ground floor landing.

Emma walked down a floor. "Nothing, Mr. Ferelli. Just trying to show Natalie that the stain is harmless."

He ascended a floor. "Why's everyone talking about the stain? *The stain this. The stain that.* I've had enough of it. I'm trying my best to keep this place clean. It's not easy doing it all by myself."

Then hire a maintenance man, she thought. "I'm sure you're doing your best. Sorry to disturb you," she said.

He waved a hand and descended the stairs. "S'all right. Just keep it down next time."

"Thank you, Mr. Ferelli," she said and gave Natalie an angry stare.

Natalie's lips pursed in protest. She exited to the hallway.

Emma sighed and made her way up the stairs. "Choose your battles," she told herself.

Emma held the tattered sweater up to the bathroom light, deciding whether to throw it in the hamper or the trash can. Natalie splashed in the soapy bubble bath.
    "Mama, do you think the monster can climb up the bath drain?"
    "What?" Emma said before she really heard the question. "No, Nattie. The monster can't come up the drain because there is no monster."
    Natalie splashed again. "There is too."
    Emma bit her lip. "Don't forget to wash behind your ears."
    "Why do I have to wash behind my ears?"
    "Because no one likes stinky ears."
    "Who doesn't?"
    Emma could only name one person, but she didn't: the ex-lover and deadbeat dad who left her fending for herself and Natalie. The son of a bitch.
    She walked to the kitchen, crumpling the sweater into a large ball before she shoved it into the plastic trash can. She stood on her toes to open the top cabinet and reached through bags and boxes of flour and cake mix till her fingers felt the cool glass of the tequila bottle.

"Mommy can't go with you. I have a lot of work to do," Emma said, repositioning blocks of text and graphics around the computer screen with the drag of a mouse.

Natalie tugged on Emma's sleeve. "Don't make me go by myself," Natalie pleaded.

Emma spun around in her swivel chair to face Natalie. "Yesterday you were a big girl. Now you need me to hold your hand?"

Natalie looked down. "That was before I saw *it*."

Emma sighed. It broke her heart to say the words. "Big girls don't tell stories, either. Or believe in monsters."

Big girls. Was she so willing to tear her daughter's childhood away so soon? She'd already told her there were no knights in shining armor. No Prince Charmings. Now there were no monsters or magic, either? What else would she tear from her? The Easter Bunny? Tooth Fairy? Santa Claus? God?

"Okay," Natalie said, but the word was hollow.

She pulled the door open.

"Remember what Mommy told you," said Emma.

Natalie turned back. "`If no one is at the bus stop, come back.'"

"Good girl. I'll see you after school."

"'Kay," Natalie said and pulled the door shut behind her.

Emma hung her head and massaged her temples.

Natalie pushed the stairwell door open and peeked through. The stain had spread all the way up and around the hinges of the door. She clung to the rail of the stair and skipped down the steps, eyeing the wall for any sign of movement.

When she reached the bottom floor she heard grownups talking. She peeked over the rail to see Mr. Ferelli, the landlord, on his knees with a host of cleaning supplies at his side.

He plunged a sponge into a bucket of soapy water, gave it a single wring that ran dirty gray, then scrubbed away at the stubborn stain on the wall and floor. Looking over his shoulder, acting as supervisor with her hands on her big, wide hips was old Mrs. Gardner, a fat white woman in a floral muumuu.

"Put some elbow grease into it. Ain't you got no elbow grease?" she asked, though it was more of a taunt.

He scrubbed harder, faster, not because it would work, but to prove it wouldn't.

Natalie bounced down the last few steps, relieved to find Antwon and Cherise waiting at the door. "Hi, Twon. Hi, Reesie."

"Hey, Nattie," they replied.

She glanced aside. "Where's Braden?"

"He scared of the ghost, so his mama drove him to school," said Antwon.

Natalie looked over her shoulder at the grownups working away on the rust stain. "What about Kanisha?"

"She's in the hospital," said Cherise. "Mama said she'll be out of school for a week."

"Are you scared of the ghost?" asked Natalie.

Antwon nodded.

"Mama said if it comes after us to rebuke it in the name of Jesus," said Cherise.

"Will that work?" Natalie asked.

"It has to," said Cherise. "Every knee shall bow at the name of Jesus. Even ghosts."

Antwon shook his head. "I don't care. I see a ghost, I'm running."

"Can I walk with you from now on?" Natalie asked.

Brother and sister faced one another in a brief, silent congress, then nodded.

"Yeah," said Cherise.

"But we can't go all the way to your floor," Antwon clarified. "We'll wait on our floor and walk down with you. And when we come back we'll walk with you up to our floor."

Natalie smiled. "Thanks."

The siblings smiled back.

Honk!

Antwon held the door for the two girls, then followed them to the waiting bus.

"Good Lord, that about gave me a heart attack," said Mrs. Gardner, staring at the leaving bus. "Does she have to honk the horn so loud every time?"

Mr. Ferelli wore a gloating smile, thankful for the distraction. Unfortunately, Mrs. Gardner quickly returned her attention to supervising the quality of his work.

"What else you got in that bucket? Try something else," she suggested.

With a sigh he lamented that the distraction had been so short-lived. He dropped the worn-out rag into the bucket, reached for a clear plastic bottle of blue liquid and sprayed it on the stain.

She laughed. "That's window cleaner. That's not gonna touch it. You know what you need?"

He turned to her and snapped. "No. What do I need?"

"Rust remover. Ain't you got no rust remover?"

He sifted through his bucket of bottles. "No, I don't."

"Are you sure? Look again."

He did so only to amuse her. "No rust remover."

"Well, that's silly. Why don't you have no rust remover? How in the world you gonna have all them bottles and not one of them is rust remover? Don't you know what you're doing?"

"I'll go to the store and get a bottle," he said, slowly rising to his feet.

She laughed. "You're gonna need more than a bottle. Look at the size of that thing," she said, pointing at the monstrous stain.

He gazed up. It seemed even bigger than when he started cleaning. He hated to admit it, but she might be right. He took a bucket in each hand and squeezed past her toward his office near the back entrance.

She waddled alongside him. "That crackpot plumber is the one who caused all this."

"What plumber?"

"That fellow you called to work on the pipes."

"Why would I do that? I take care of the maintenance," he said, the water sloshing in the bucket and the key ring jangling on his belt.

She shrugged. "Maybe it was Hilda. God rest her soul."

"Mrs. Eckhart? She wouldn't do that."

"Wish you could ask her. Too bad she slipped on the wet stairs."

He placed the buckets down and fiddled with the keys. "The stairs are not wet."

She pointed back to the landing. "Then why's that sign say WET FLOOR?"

"So I don't get sued by crazy tenants like you."

"Do you think you'll have it all fixed by--"

The door slammed shut in her face. With a frown she turned and waddled back to the stairs. "It was too the plumber," she mumbled.

The children entered the lobby that afternoon to find Mr. Ferelli setting up shop just beneath the stairs for a second round of stain-fighting. As before, one bucket was full of soapy water; the other, this time, was full of small brown bottles of rust remover.

Antwon, Cherise and Natalie ascended the stairs in tight formation, their hands on the rail.

When they reached the fourth floor landing, they stopped.

"Sorry we can't go with you," said Cherise.

"Thanks, anyway," said Natalie. "But you'll wait for me tomorrow?"

The siblings nodded.

"Good luck," Antwon said and opened the door for his sister. He waved and pulled the door shut behind him.

Natalie looked up the towering series of stairs. She exhaled and skipped up the stairs as fast as she could.

Down below, Mr. Ferelli opened the bottle of rust remover and sprayed the base of the stain. There was a strange cry, like an injured animal. Mr. Ferelli glanced about for a moment, then took the sponge from the bucket and scrubbed away at the stain. The cry came again.

He ignored it and returned the sponge to the bucket and retrieved the rust remover. He sprayed the wall again, only to have the acidic spray bounce off the wall straight into his eyes.

"Oh God!" he yelled and immediately took the sponge from the soapy bucket and washed his closed eyes.

The spreading branches of the stain, surrounding the now bleach-white spot, parted from the wall; like spidery legs, they closed upon Mr. Ferelli's face with an awful searing sound.

He leaped back, falling out of the clutches of the monster and into the bucket. Its dirty gray contents spilled over and spread across the lobby floor. All the while he screamed, "My eyes! My eyes!"

The neighbors gathered in the stairwell, watching as the EMTs carefully raised Mr. Ferelli onto the wheeled stretcher. Red, white and blue lights splashed onto the lobby walls like some patriotic light show, but there was no rejoicing. No hands over hearts--they were over gaping mouths, over horrified eyes.

The top of Mr. Ferelli's face and head were bandaged with gauze, but not enough to cover the strange white patches where olive skin had been stripped of color.

"I can't see. Oh God, I can't see. The thing attacked me. It burned my face," he said between sobs.

"Is he all right?" Gloria asked.

"He's in shock. We'll have him stabilized soon," said the EMT pushing the stretcher to the back of the ambulance.

Antwon, Cherise and Natalie watched way up from the fourth floor landing, barred by protective mothers from getting a closer look. Two floors above them, Braden looked down.

"Will he be okay?" Emma asked the EMT.

"We'll perform another eye wash and take him to the ER right away."

"What about his face? What happened to his skin?" she asked, but the EMT only shrugged. "Poor man," she said.

"Lord, have mercy. He's half out of his mind," Gloria whispered. "I hope this doesn't give the children nightmares."

The mothers looked up at the curious children, who peeked over the rail like perching birds hungry for gory details.

"Are Antwon and Cherise going on about a monster?" Emma asked.

"They keep talking about ghosts. Why, does Natalie?"

"She says the stain on the wall is a monster."

Gloria looked over her shoulder. "She's not lying. That thing is a beast."

Emma laughed until the sobering reality resurfaced. "Seriously. If she keeps going on, I don't know what I'm going to do with her. Or myself. Last night I went on a date with Jose Cuervo."

Gloria's eyes widened in surprise. "Girl," she said, drawing out the word.

"I know. The last thing I need is Social Services checking in on me and finding me drunk or stuck with a hangover. But it's seriously too much. It's beginning to drive me crazy."

"You're doing a good job, Emma. You don't have anything to worry about. I'll vouch for you any time."

"Thank you, Gloria. But after Kanisha's accident I think they're really suspicious."

"You don't have to tell me. I've seen their cars parked across the street," said Gloria, placing a hand on her hip and shaking her head with a huff. "Think I don't know what a government car looks like. That's one of them there," she pointed.

Emma looked through the open door to the white car across the street. A circular seal graced the door, but was too far to make out its design or the accompanying text. "Is that Social Services?" she asked.

Gloria shrugged. "Who else would it be?"

"Let's get moving before they come ask more questions," Emma said and began her ascent.

Gloria followed, a bit slower with her heavier frame. "You already talked to them?"

"Did they call you, too?"

"You mean for Monique's `character reference'?"

Emma's eyes lit. "They *did* call you. What did you tell them?"

"I'm not a snitch. Besides, she's not a bad mother. A hoochie, maybe, but not a bad mother."

Emma sighed. "You're right. I said the same thing. Minus the hoochie part. Or the bitch part."

They laughed.

"Why are y'all laughing?" Cherise asked when the women came to the fourth floor landing.

"Oh. We weren't laughing about Mr. Ferelli. We were laughing about something else," Emma said, cradling Natalie's back with a palm. "You kids have a good night. Night, Gloria."

The siblings waved.

"Good night, Emma. Night, Natalie," Gloria echoed and opened the door for the children to exit.

Natalie hurried to the far side of the stairs and took her mother's right hand. "Mama," she said, tugging at Emma's coat as they ascended the stairs.

"What, baby?"

"Can we move back home?"

"What? No, baby. This is home."

"I don't wanna live here anymore."

"Why not?"

"The monster."

"There is no monster, baby. Mr. Ferelli just got chemicals in his eyes. He should have worn glasses to protect his eyes but he didn't. That's what happens when you work with chemicals without protecting your hands and eyes. You can get burned real bad. That's all it is. But if they catch it in time, they can help him see again."

"They'll catch the monster in time?"

"No, honey, I meant the burn. If they catch the burn in time they can save his eyes."

"Did they catch the burn in time?"

"I don't know, baby. I sure hope so."

"Me, too."

Natalie looked back at the stain. She was sure, beneath the noise of the EMTs, the gossiping neighbors, and Mr. Ferelli's painful cries, she had heard another cry, one of a wounded animal, and yet now the cry began to sound remarkably like a scared and angry growl.

Emma stopped to listen. Her brow furrowed.

Natalie's eyes widened. "Do you hear it, Mama?"

Emma released Natalie's hand and raised a finger to her lips in hush. She turned her head left and right, tilted it to catch the sound. Her eyes rolled. "Somebody has a dog. Mr. Ferelli wouldn't like that, bless his heart."

Natalie's hopeful eyes shrunk to pitiful, dark circles. Emma took her by the hand again and ascended the stairs.

The door to the long hall opened. Emma gave Natalie a gentle nudge to exit their apartment, then pulled the door shut behind them. She pulled her purse strap snug to her shoulder and took a step forward, when she noticed Natalie had dug her heels into the thin carpet, refusing to budge.

Natalie tugged on Emma's shirttail. "Mama?"

Emma looked into her eyes. "What is it, honey?"

"The monster," Natalie pointed at the stained ceiling outside the stairwell. "It climbed up the stairs."

"Honey, it's just a water stain. When the pipes leak too long it makes an ugly stain. That's all it is."

Natalie didn't see any pipes on their floor. Maybe they were above the ceiling, but it didn't ease her fear. "It is *too* a monster. It's the one that scraped off Kanisha's face and hurt Mr. Ferelli's eyes."

"No, honey. That was from the chemicals Mr. Ferelli used."

"He didn't use them on Kanisha."

"He sprayed them on the wall. She touched the wall and rubbed her face. That's what hurt her."

Even as Emma heard the words come out of her own mouth, she doubted their validity. Could Kanisha have gotten so much of the chemical on her face as to bleach her flesh? It didn't matter. The idea that a monster was occupying their apartment building was ridiculous.

Emma gave Natalie a second nudge. "Come on. Let's go so you don't miss your bus."

Natalie shook her head. "Don't make me go," she whimpered.

"Honey, I'll be right beside you. The Boogeyman isn't going to get you."

"No."

"Natalie, you have to go to school. You know the elevator doesn't work so we have to use the stairs. I use them every day. Has anything happened to me?"

Of course Natalie knew nothing had happened to her mother. But that didn't mean it hadn't happened to Kanisha and Mr. Ferelli.

"Please, Mom?" she asked.

"Hold Mommy's hand. You'll be fine," Emma said, biting her lip as she took Natalie's left hand in her own and proceeded down the hall.

Natalie's steps staggered as she alternately tried to stop and keep up with her mother. When they entered the stairwell, Natalie wrestled her hand free and swapped sides with her mother, so that Emma stood between her and the wall and the ugly amorphous monster across it.

They exited the lobby onto the sidewalk, where they waited the short while with the other children and parents until the school bus arrived. The orange-yellow door contracted to give way.

Emma gave Natalie a kiss on the forehead. "Hope you have a good day. Mommy's going to run some errands and will see you when you get home. 'kay?"

Natalie nodded.

"Good girl," Emma said and rubbed her back. "Love you."

"Love you, too," Natalie said and boarded the bus behind the other children.

Emma pushed the stairwell door open and stepped onto the eighth floor with a brown paper bag full of groceries in one arm. She turned back and retrieved a second bag from the stairwell landing. When she glanced down the hall at her apartment, she couldn't help but notice the ugly stain had spread considerably.

She followed the stain down the hallway, past neighboring apartments. The stain meandered from ceiling to wall, above a doorframe and back to the ceiling, then back down the wall until another door impeded its path.

She traced the path to her own apartment door, where it simply vanished where the wall and ceiling met. After placing her grocery bags on the floor and entering her passcode, she pulled the door open.

She took both bags in her hands and placed them on the opposite side of the door, then stepped across the threshold, daring to look up.

The bus door opened and gushed forth four children onto the sidewalk. They entered the apartment stairwell and made their way up the stairs, clinging to the far right of the stairs, at first walking at a quiet, slow pace. The higher they climbed, the faster they walked, until they broke one after the other into a stair-step-leaping run.

Brother and sister exited through the fourth floor door and Braden the sixth, leaving Natalie to run the last two flights to her floor. She exited the stairwell to find the stain had crawled from where she stood, across the ceiling and down the hall, all in the span of a school day.

She clung to the wall on the elevator side as she advanced, for no logical reason but that perhaps she could enter the broken elevator for refuge should the stain attack, though she knew full well the electronic doors had been deactivated.

She reached her apartment, entered the passcode and pulled the door open. The room was empty, save two bags of groceries resting upon the floor. She stepped inside and gazed up at the bloody-brown stain. She swallowed nervously.

"Mom?" she called.

Natalie expected her to come out of the kitchen and greet her. She cornered the living room and dining room into the empty kitchen, then circled back to the living room and walked down the hall, ever mindful of the red stain clinging to the ceiling above her. It stopped just short of the bathroom.

Back hunched, she traversed the hall to avoid any arms of the monster should they suddenly dangle down and grab her. When she reached the bathroom, she found the door cracked open. Peeking through the narrow sliver, she saw a pair of legs on the floor.

Natalie took a deep breath and reached for the knob, afraid to see what lay on the other side of the door. She carefully pulled the knob to avoid the door creaking, lest it alert the monster above to her presence, if it was not already aware.

Emma's upper half was crammed into the cabinet beneath the sink, as if it had swallowed her. Natalie held her breath, terrified at the sight. The legs twitched. The feet, pointed down, walked backwards, until her mother emerged from the cabinet with a brown plastic bottle in her hand.

Emma noticed a ghost-white Natalie standing quietly in the doorway. "Hey, kiddo. You okay?"

Natalie released the captive breath. "You scared me, Mom!"

"How did I do that, scaredy cat?"

"Mom!"

"I'm just teasing," Emma said and reached overhead, fumbling atop the sink for the white cap. When she found it, she placed it atop the bottle.

"Is that the stuff that hurts the monster?"

"I told you, honey--it's not a monster. It's a water stain. And the only way to remove it is to spray it with the right stuff."

Natalie glanced at her feet then faced Emma. "Can we spray it on the stain?"

"Only Mommy can use it, because it's acid. Acid means it's very strong. It's the stuff that hurt Kanisha and Mr. Ferelli. So don't play with it. Understand?"

Natalie stared at the brown plastic bottle. It seemed awfully small. How could something so small hurt someone so bad? It wasn't nearly as scary as the monster on the walls.

"Honey, did you hear Mommy?" Emma asked.

Natalie nodded. "Yes, ma'am."

Emma smiled. "Good. And don't you worry about that monster. We'll spray him in the eyes and make him real sorry."

Natalie's unsure eyes wandered off.

Emma stood from the floor and placed the bottle atop the sink. "But we'll have to take care of him in a minute. For now I need you to help me put up the groceries, 'kay?"

Natalie faced her mother and nodded.

"Good girl," Emma said and reached to cup Natalie's face.

Natalie shrunk back from her mother's touch.

"What?" Emma asked.

Natalie pointed at the bottle.

"Oh, guess I should wash my hands first, huh?"

Natalie nodded.

Emma knocked on the closed bedroom door. "Natty, you feeling okay?"

"Yes, ma'am," a soft voice answered from the other side.

"Have you finished your homework?"

"Yes, ma'am."

"Don't you want to watch cartoons? They're still on."

"No, ma'am."

Emma was confused. Natalie always watched cartoons after homework, and if she didn't have homework you could hardly peel her off the couch or the remote from her hands.

"You sure you're feeling okay?" Emma tried again.

"Yes, ma'am," Natalie answered, staring at the ceiling above the door.

Soft footsteps faded to silence. At present there was no sign of intrusion by the ugly monster, but Natalie knew it was coming. She sat against the headboard of her bed, clutching the blankets to take cover under at any moment.

She would stay in her room until the monster was removed, as her mother promised, at least she hoped—but the pressure of her burning bladder was getting heavier, and soon one would have to give.

Natalie could still remember the last time she had peed her bed. She was six. Daddy raised a fuss and hit her with the back of his hand—the same part of his hand Mommy had caught for some reason once and for some reason forgave once, on the condition it never happen to either of them again. That's when she and Mommy left Daddy and never looked back.

She could also still remember Daddy holding her white bed sheet up into the light to emphasize the ugly yellow stain, dangling it before her in condemnation as if she didn't know what she had done. Of course she knew, she'd woken up crying in the cold musty puddle after all.

And soon, the monster stain would come crawling on the wall through her door, or above on her ceiling and dangle before her, condemning her to permanent blindness and eternal darkness. Would it strike her cheek clean of color as it had Kanisha? Or purple and blue the way Daddy did?

All the memories of peeing her bed only made the need to relieve herself stronger. She knew Mommy wouldn't hit her for having an accident, but she knew it wouldn't be an accident if she just sat there and let nature take its course.

She carefully pushed her blankets aside and crawled to the edge of her mattress, knowing full well this monster was not one to hide undetected beneath beds, but boldly stood out in plain sight, challenging all to fear it. Still, her bed provided a type of comfort and refuge she wasn't anxious to leave.

The needles in her bladder demanded she take action, so she stepped onto the floor and hurried to her door. When she opened it, she saw the stain had advanced into the bathroom. A fearful grimace fell upon her face. She crossed her legs and held her crotch, until a warm dribble escaped.

She swallowed her fear and walked tight-legged to the bathroom, staring at the stain looming overhead. She dropped her garments and sat on the toilet to relieve herself.

Like a magnet her eyes were drawn to the ceiling. She expected the stain to move at any moment. Could such fear give it life? Would it? The sheer thought compelled her to close her eyes and focus solely on the sound of her emptying bladder. Slowly—too slowly--the needles came out, the nagging pressure subsided, and she was empty.

She pulled up her pants and flushed the toilet. How it roared. She turned the water on to wash her hands, focusing on her reflection in the mirror to avoid seeing the monster stain above her. In the corner of her vision she perceived movement. Or was it her imagination? Or would her imagination power the thing's movement?

The roaring continued. She looked at the toilet. It had already emptied and was nearly full. Yet the roaring.

Don't look, she told herself. *Don't turn around,* she thought. But it *was* moving. The stain was reaching down, just as anxious for her as she imagined it would be, and like an angry unreasoning animal, it growled.

"Mom!" she yelled and dropped to her knees.

"What's the matter?" Emma's voice came from down the hall, accompanied by the sound of hurried footsteps.

Natalie crawled to the tub to avoid the stain's reach.

"Oh my god!" Emma shouted, observing with her own eyes the animate stain's flat, misshapen limb reaching down for her daughter.

Natalie turned around to crawl to her mother, when just as quickly, Emma ran away.

"No, Mama!" Natalie shouted.

The limb swiped at her.

She screamed.

"Cover your eyes!" Emma shouted, having returned with the

bottle of rust remover.

Natalie closed her eyes and shielded her face with her arms.

Emma squeezed the bottle, spraying the stain with a jet of acid.

The mouthless thing screamed, from where surely no vocal cords existed—a shriek of pain, betrayal, hatred and hunger. The wounded limb retreated toward the ceiling.

"Come to Mommy," said Emma, but Natalie had curled into a ball to shield herself from harm. "Hurry, Nattie, quickly."

From behind Emma, another limb shot down and struck her back. She screamed in pain, instinctively reaching back to survey the damage. The singed edge of the hole in her shirt exposed a white welt she couldn't see. She spun about and gave the bottle another squeeze, dousing the ceiling and dangling limb with a dose of acid.

Another ear-piercing shriek came from the creature. Emma placed the bottle on the sink and stooped over to take hold of Natalie.

"Come on, honey, stand up," Emma said, helping her daughter to her feet. "Let's get out of here."

They turned to leave the bathroom when limb after limb descended from the ceiling to the floor, forming a series of brown, acid bars. Emma humored the possibility she and Natalie could squeeze between and around the bleaching bars, but the thought of their flesh being seared and stripped of pigment was stronger.

"Get inside the tub," Emma said and gave Natalie a push.

Natalie covered her head with her arms and climbed into the tub. Emma did likewise, shielding her daughter from the limbs that lashed out. Another burning swipe at her arm caused her to collapse upon her daughter.

"Ow, Mommy!" shouted Natalie, unable to move.

Emma pulled the vinyl shower curtain closed and watched the limbs strike it again and again, expecting it to be torn to shreds, yet it remained intact.

She sat on her knees, allowing Natalie room to squirm about beneath her.

"Mom?" said Natalie.

"What is it, honey?"

"It's coming in."

"Where, honey?" Emma asked, looking at the white ceramic tub surrounding them.

Natalie pointed up.

Emma gazed at the ceiling. The stain was slowly advancing. Already, tiny limbs the size of fingers were extending, wriggling with life like hungry worms, growing longer, descending lower with each passing second.

"Oh God, no!" Emma said, covering Natalie's face with an arm.

She took hold of the shower curtain and yanked it, pulling it free from half a dozen rings before the entire shower rod came falling on top of her.

"Stay beneath the curtain," she said and pulled it over them. "Make sure your legs don't stick out."

Natalie curled into a fetal ball. Likewise, Emma curled up beneath the curtain, tucking it beneath her legs and Natalie's head.

"If we stay under here it can't hurt us," she said, unsure of her own words.

Within seconds, a thousand limbs came showering upon them as rapid as raindrops, pelting the thick shower curtain like a beating drum, yet the acid fingers were unable to penetrate the protective shield.

Natalie's cries dug deeper than any chemical knives possibly could.

"Shh," said Emma. "I'm right here, baby. I won't let them get you."

She held her daughter tight, until the unrelenting rain lulled them both to exhaustion, and finally to sleep.

A loud sound woke Natalie from her peaceful slumber back to the nightmare reality. From her confined position, she scanned her surroundings. All was veiled in hazy white.

They were still beneath the curtain. It appeared intact. The pounding assault and hammering sound had ceased. Her mother's hand lay in front of her, motionless.

"Mama?" she called.

No answer.

She tried to roll over, but the dead weight of her mother upon her made it impossible.

"Mom, I can't move," she said, but there was no response.

She squirmed about, grunted, tried to push her mother's hands away from her.

"Mom!" she yelled.

With a gasp, Emma came to, instinctively squeezing her tight. "What?" she asked.

"Let go," growled Natalie. "I can't move."

Emma surveyed their surroundings. When she perceived the attack was over, she loosened her hold upon Natalie.

"I heard a noise," said Natalie.

Emma listened to the silence. "No, I think it's over, honey."

"But I heard something."

Emma listened again. There was a bang. A crash. Somewhere close enough to hear but not to distinguish.

Then silence once more.

"Mama?" said Natalie.

"What, honey?"

"I'm thirsty."

Emma sat up just enough to gaze upon her daughter's face. Her eyes were red from crying herself to sleep, her lips pale and dry. Emma ran a finger over her own lips, cracked like unsanded wood. How long had they been asleep?

She reached over Natalie's head till the shower curtain pulled from under them and grew taut. She took hold of the cold water handle and turned it. A low creak sounded and a gasp of air escaped the faucet, but not a drip came out.

"Where's the water, Mama?" Natalie asked.

Emma contemplated the possibilities, resolving upon one. "They cut it off."

"Who cut it off?"

"I don't know. I think somebody knows about the--" she hesitated to say it, but there was no other word for it. "--monster."

"Somebody knows we're here?" Natalie asked, a twinkle of hope in her dark eyes.

"I think so, honey." The words, even if they weren't true, gave her hope as she spoke them.

"Maybe the monster's gone," said Natalie.

"Let's just be quiet, and listen."

Their breaths sounded back and forth, each inhaling, exhaling, when the other wasn't. Without verbal agreement, they ordered their breaths to gradually align, and with a bit of selective hearing they both heard nothing but the silence of the dead apartment building.

Then a sound, closer. A rumble. A crash. A shout. Shout?

Other voices joined. Angry voices, ordering. Male and female. A horrible roar like old, creaking pipes, followed by a man's scream. A hissing sound. It grew louder, joined with movement. Feet stomping.

Natalie's tiny heart pounded louder than her mother's. The perfect steps of their dancing breaths became staggered. Natalie breathed louder until the breaths became gasps, then whimpers.

"Shh, honey, shh," said Emma, herself afraid.

Her hand slipped around Natalie's mouth. She didn't want to muzzle her daughter, but it might soon be necessary.

"Clear!" a man's voice shouted.

The hissing sound again. Another roar. A woman's yelp of pain.

"I'm okay," the woman said.

"Clear!" someone shouted, this time louder.

A loud roar, just over Emma and Natalie. They screamed. The hissing sounded, just before the shower curtain was ripped off the two bathtub prisoners.

Emma looked over her shoulder. An arm, covered in some protective material, reached out to her.

"We found two!" someone shouted.

"Give me your hand," said a man behind the clear screen of his HAZMAT helmet. It, the suit, gloves and boots were all made of the same material.

Emma extended her hand, and with little effort was pulled to her feet. Another soldier came behind him. She reached into the tub and pulled Natalie into her arms.

"It's all right, baby. I got you," said the masked woman.

"Is there anyone else in the apartment, ma'am?" the man asked Emma, but before she could answer, another voice shouted, "Clear!"

Emma was jerked by the strong hand out of the bathroom. As the small group of soldiers led her down the hall, out of the living room into the main hall, all she could do was glance back over her shoulder at the woman carrying Natalie.

"Eyes ahead! I have your daughter," said the woman.

Emma reluctantly obeyed. Beyond the man leading her by the hand were two more suited soldiers, the foremost with a backpack and long gun, and the other with his hand to his earpiece, communicating every maneuver.

Natalie could only stare over the shoulder of the woman carrying her, like a child in the backseat of a car facing the rear windshield. The man following her held a long gun that sprayed something at the monster—it must have been the same stuff her mother had used.

Whatever it was, it caused the monster tremendous agony. It roared in reaction, all the while swiping at any living thing with its flat, amorphous appendages.

Her kicked-in apartment door became a tiny rectangle. The big brown stain above had large wounds of white where the ceiling showed through. The group entered the stairwell, the man still spraying the hissing gun at the monster above when the door shut behind them all.

Hard-bottomed boots clanked on the metal stairs, echoing all around. The group descended, floor after floor, all the while dodging the swiping limbs and countering with blasts from their spray guns.

A scream.

Natalie turned her head as far as it would go, only to see a nearly naked man pulled up into the ceiling. His helmet and suit lay on the ground. Next to his dangling earpiece, his feet kicked frantically until a shower of blood rained over the fleeing fugitives. Natalie wanted to scream, but nothing came out.

Before they turned the corner to the next floor, she saw the man's legs pulled up into the stain. The soldier looked like a cartoon character flattened by a steamroller. His parts swirled around each other on the ceiling like a bowl full of melted Neapolitan, pink and white and brown.

The man in back shot a spray of acid at the monster. It rattled and roared like the old pipes running up and down the stairwell. Natalie shook her arm to sling the spatters of blood off.

"Hold still, baby, we're almost there," said the woman carrying her.

"Where's Mama?" Natalie asked.

"She's right ahead of us."

Natalie could only think of the man *right ahead* of them only seconds ago, now a bloody puddle of ceiling soup. "Mama?" she called.

Emma turned back. "Natalie?"

"Mama?"

"Keep moving, ma'am," said the man holding Emma's hand.

"Your daughter is safe," said the woman carrying Natalie.

They reached the bottom landing. Natalie looked at the wall where the stain had begun, now white and completely free of the monster, as the bottom few floors had been.

"Go, go, go!" said the man with the spray gun in front, allowing the soldiers carrying Emma and Natalie to exit the building first.

The two armed soldiers backed out of the stairwell last.

Outside it was gray, but bright and welcoming. Even the dirty diesel city air smelled good. Emma and Natalie took deep gushing breaths of it.

A dozen neighbors stood on the crowded sidewalk comforting one another. Gloria and Monique embraced, weeping, but safe.

The two men with saggy pants, who always stood by the porch smoking cigarettes and chatting, now sat on the curb, their bare black arms and shoulders covered in white welts. They hovered over Antwon, Cherise, and Braden like mother hens, running off the news-hungry wolves with microphones and cameras and voice recorders.

The street was occupied by military and emergency vehicles, in addition to two of the white cars Emma and Gloria had seen earlier. Suited agents stood just beside the cars, radios tucked behind their ears as they communicated with unseen superiors.

The soldier escorting Emma released her hand. The one carrying Natalie lowered her to the sidewalk. Mother and daughter embraced one another with tears of joy.

They were free. They were alive.

Emma and Natalie sat side by side on the concrete curb, sharing a blanket the EMTs had provided to prevent shock. Neighbors spoke with police and others, giving accounts of their encounter with the monster. Natalie hated each time the authorities used the term "creature" or "entity." What was an entity, anyway?

Emma looked around several times, counting heads, assigning names to faces, but Mrs. Gardner and Cindy were nowhere in sight. She brushed Natalie's hair out of her face and smiled. Natalie leaned into Emma. Mother was warm--warm and good and safely reassuring.

The sounds of conversation, sirens coming and going, and the distant noise of the busy city grew silent in Natalie's ears. Only her breathing and her mother's beating heart remained. She shoved them deep beneath the ringing of her ears.

A drip sounded, piercing the calm. She looked to her side, where a metal grate fed into the city's sewer system. A small stream of water ran from somewhere uptown, all the way down her side of the imperceptibly bowed street, along the curb, right to the grate.

It must have rained while we were inside, she thought.

The sky was gray, after all. That was a sure sign of rain coming or going.

Drip-drip.
Drip-drip.
She blinked.
Drip-drip.
Blink.
Drip-drip.
Blink-blink.

She found herself blinking in time with each drop. Her shoulders trembled, as though each breaking droplet were a freezing downpour of gray sky rain pouring over her. Fear drenched her, soaked her to the chilling bone, body shivering and teeth chattering. Her aching heart pounded and stopped, pounded and stopped, all in time with the water dripping at her feet.

A.P. SESSLER

A resident of North Carolina's Outer Banks, A.P. frequents an alternate universe not too different from your own, where he searches for that unique element that twists the everyday commonplace into the weird. When he's not writing fiction, he composes music, makes art and muses about theology and mind-hacking. He also likes to dress in funny clothes and talk about the first English colony in the New World.